BEING THE FIRST PART OF HAEE AND THE OTHER MIDDLINGS

Haee

The Cat with a Crooked Tail

R.S. Vern

BEING THE FIRST PART OF HAEE AND THE OTHER MIDDLINGS

Haee

The Cat with a Crooked Tail

R.S. Vern

MIDDLING INDUSTRIES

BY R.S. VERN

ILLUSTRATED BOOK SERIES

Haee and the Other Middlings
Part I: Haee The Cat with a Crooked Tail
Part II: The Unconventional Life of Haee
Part III: Haee's Quest for the Greater Prairie

PROSE AND POEMS

Scribbles from the Middling Cat

NOVEL

The Itch of the Middling Cat

Should you wish to contact the Publisher, please send your enquiries to rights@middlingindustries.com.

Haee The Cat with a Crooked Tail
Being First Part of Haee and the Other Middlings

Digital book
ISBN 978-9-8107-0191-8
Paperback
ISBN 978-9-8118-7105-4
Hardcover
ISBN 978-9-8118-7106-1

First published 2012 as digital book
Second published 2023 as digital and print books

Illustrations by Josh C.

Published by Middling Industries
www.middlingindustries.com

Publisher's Note

This is fiction. For all ages.

If you find any similarities of yourself here, it is purely out of coincidence or a result of the author's daydreams.

Or you could just be one serious fellow middling.

Definition

Middlings commonly have a comfortable standard of living, considerable economic security, moderate work + life autonomy and often rely on their own expertise to sustain themselves.

They place great emphasis on independence, value innovation, respect the non-conformist and have great concerns for the environment. They appear established and well-rounded but, often have insecurities locked within.

Middlings live among others but essentially feel apart from it all.

They often ask themselves this: "Are we just not as happy as those who are much better off in this world?"

Preface

Looking
can make you want.

Wanting
can get you thinking.

If you want them to
stop thinking,
just give them what
they want.

Haee is a
middling cat
with an
unusually long
and crooked tail.

He has a great family who loves and dotes on him.

Haee never has much to worry about.

Like all cats,
Haee is a curious cat.

One day, he decides
to venture out.

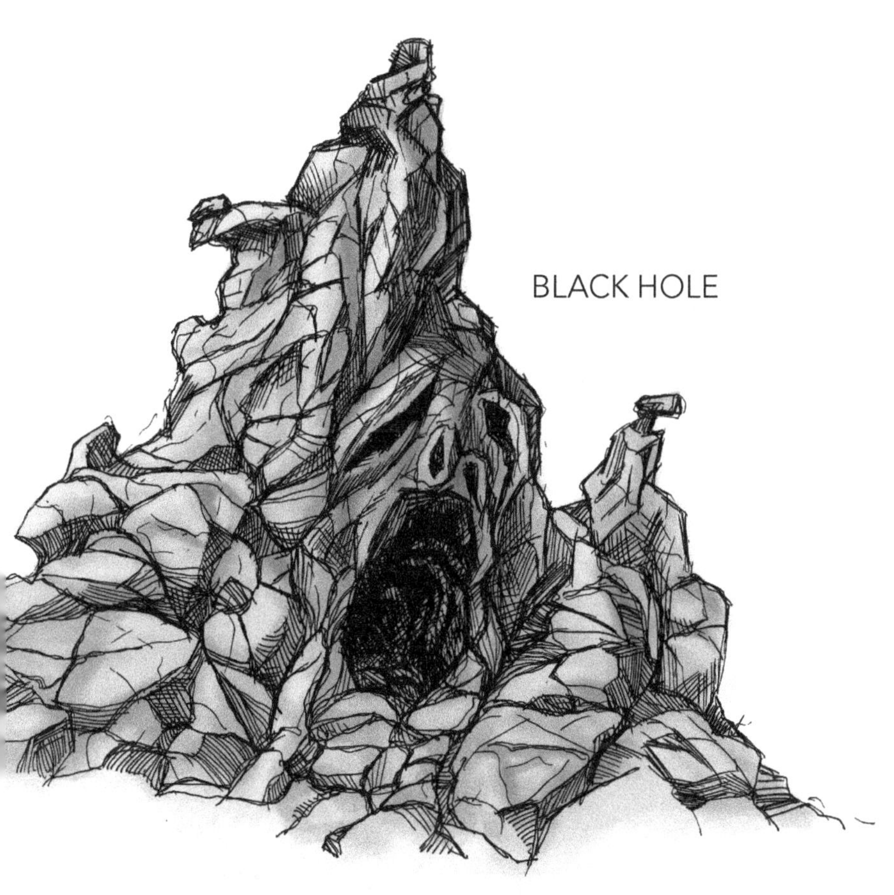

He comes across a black hole. It looks dangerous and menacing.

"Hmm…where could this lead to?"

Curious and fearless,
Haee decides to explore
the black hole.

There are several turnings in the black hole.
He decides to make a left first,
and then right at the next turn.
"There must be a special treat at the end of this!"

Haee walks for hours.

As he gets tired and hungry,
he decides to turn back.

But he can no longer
remember his way home.

"meow.....meow.....meow....."

The black hole has not
led him to any special treat.

In fact, it has become
a threat to his life.

"meow.....meow.....meow....."

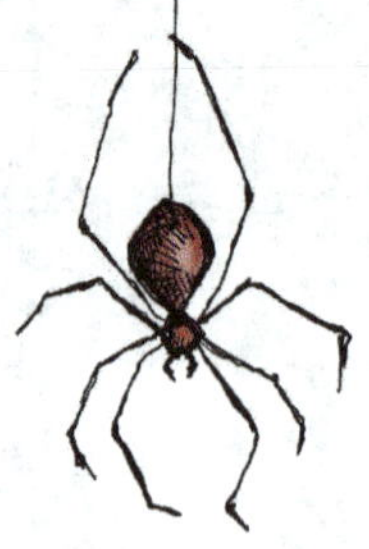

Alone and terribly afraid, he swears he will never act so foolishly and recklessly again.

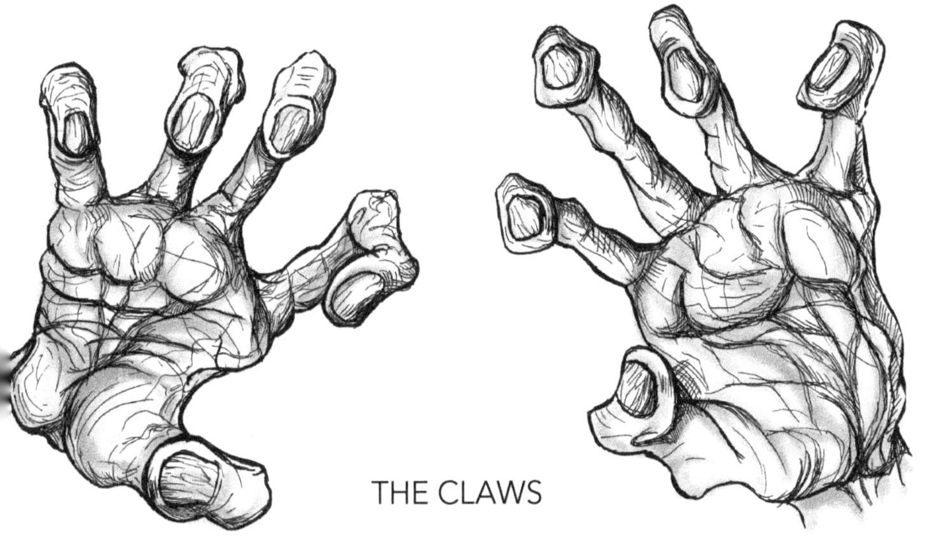

THE CLAWS

Suddenly, Haee sees a pair of huge claws coming at him!

Like the black hole, the claws look dangerous and menacing.

Terrified, Haee tries to escape.
But he is too weak to run.

The claws catch hold
of him, lifting him out
from the black hole.

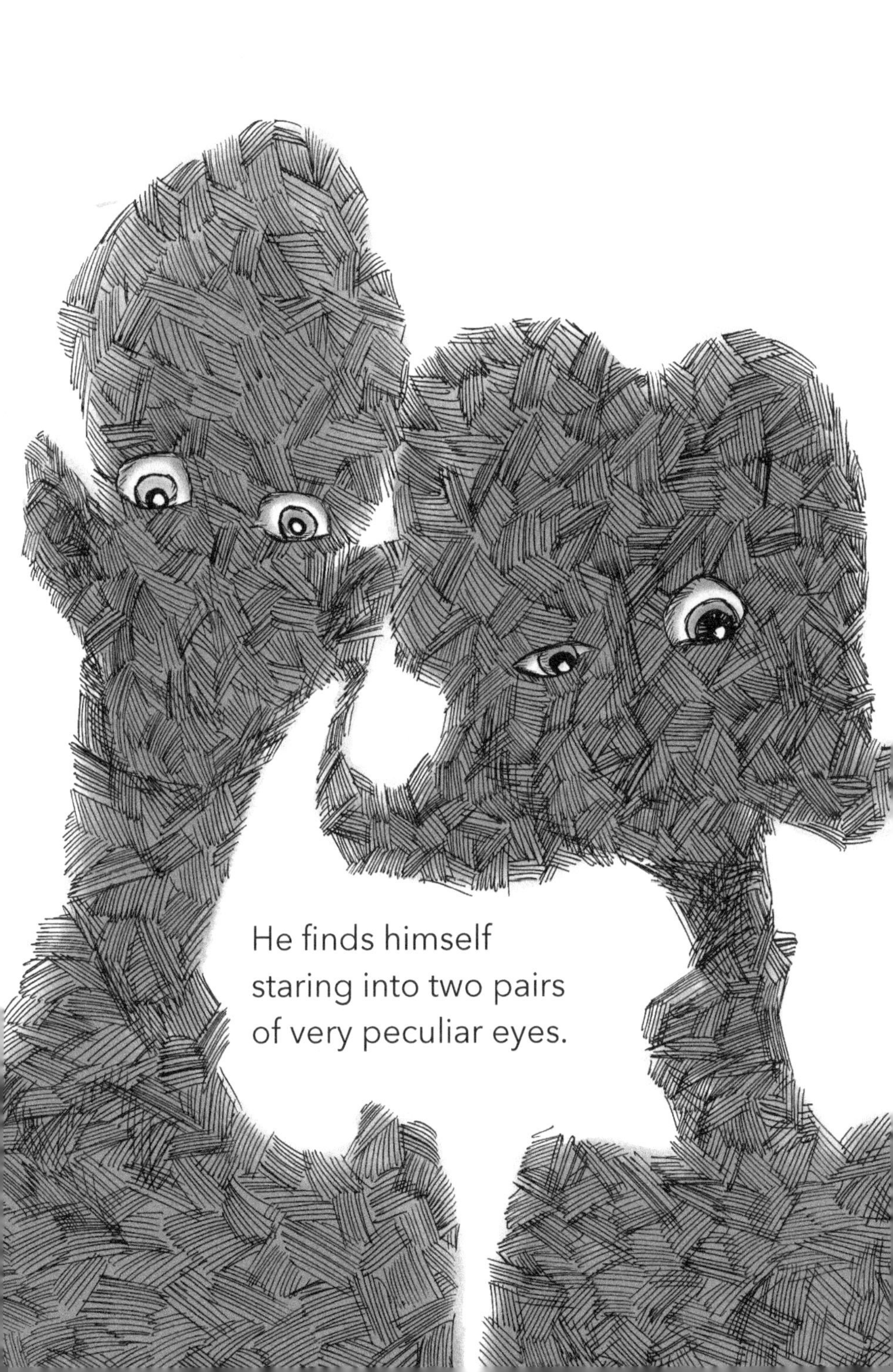

He finds himself
staring into two pairs
of very peculiar eyes.

The "claws" turn out to be his saviour. They belong to Tom, a very different middling.

Tom lives with Jane.

MIDDLINGS

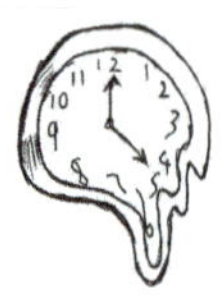

Haee begins a life with these two middlings.

They always do things together.

They sleep on the same bed and eat on the same table.

Their favourite game is hide-and-seek.

Haee leads a very comfortable and secure life with Tom and Jane.

Everything is provided for him. When he gets hungry, Jane feeds him tuna biscuits. When he gets bored, Tom plays with him.

There is nothing to worry or think about. Life is easy and carefree for him.

There are other cats in the neighbourhood.

But Haee never plays with them.

He spends his time grooming and sun-bathing. His shiny coat of fur makes him the best looking cat in the neighbourhood.

Occasionally, he gets a nightmare whenever he thinks about the black hole.

He swears never to put himself in such danger again.

Conveniently, this house becomes Haee's world. Nothing seems to exist outside of the house.

Tom and Jane are his only friends.

This carries on
for many months.

Soon, the months
become years.

Feeling bored
and restless, Haee
begins to observe his
friends, Tom and Jane.

Tom and Jane are hard working middlings. They lead a comfortable and routine life.

Everyday, they wake up early for work, go for evening jogs, and sleep early at night.

Tom is an accountant. He is meticulous with numbers and excels in what he does.

He drives a nice car and sends Jane to work every morning.

MIDDLING CITY

Tom is a strong believer in organic living.

He grows and harvests fruits and vegetables in his garden.

Sometimes, Tom tells Haee about his secret desire to lead a simple life.

He wishes he can give up everything in the city, and move somewhere where the air is clean.

But Tom can never seem to do that.

Jane is a columnist at an established global print title.

She writes on politics, finance, investment, and housing.

She recognises what she writes do not necessarily reflect what she believes in.

Jane grumbles a lot about life.
She complains to Haee about wealth, power, and politics.

Sometimes, she gets so angry she starts getting hives.

Jane secretly wishes she becomes a bird so she can fly away to see the world.

When she gets tired,
she will find a tall tree
and just perch.

Despite their secret desires to live different lives, Tom and Jane are still very happy in their own ways.

Jane even has a set of rules for Haee at home.

HOUSE RULES FOR
HAEE

- KEEP THE HOUSE CLEAN BY "TAKING CARE" OF THE HOUSE PESTS.
- PLAY WITH TOM ONLY IN THE EVENINGS.
- SLEEP ON THE BED ONLY AFTER YOU HAVE TAKEN YOUR MONTHLY SHOWER.
- EAT ONE MEAL A DAY SO YOU WILL NOT BECOME OVERWEIGHT.
- DO NOT PEE AND POO IN THE GARDEN.
- YOU CAN PEE AND POO ONLY IN YOUR POO PEN.

At first, Haee has trouble following the rules.

But he gets used to them in no time.

Haee keeps the house clean by "taking care" of the pests.

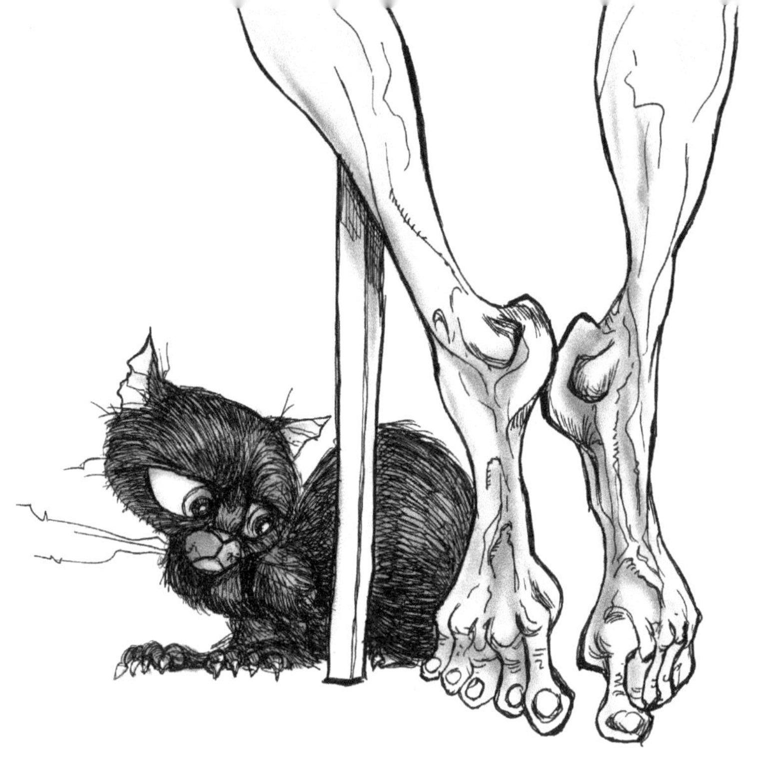

He plays with Tom
only in the evenings.

He takes his monthly shower and eats one meal a day.

Haee pees and poos in his poo pen.

He gets rewarded with treats for being such an obedient cat.

Over time, Haee gets
bored and restless again.

He sits by the window and
starts to wonder about the
world outside.

He thinks about his encounter with the black hole.

“hmm......”

Finally, he decides to venture out of his comfortable home.

Haee gets to know new friends in the back alley.

There is a cat he especially loves hanging out with.

Her name is Whie.

Whie has an unusually big red nose that almost covers her entire face.

Whie does not have any friend or family because of her big red nose.

Every cat makes fun of her, except Haee.

When Haee gets special treats from Jane, he shares them with Whie.

Haee enjoys being with Whie so much that, he decides to stay with Whie in the alley.

Haee stops going back to Tom and Jane's house.

Addendum

On a Rare Sitting with R.S. Vern

Haee interviews R.S. Vern in a rare sitting at home. This is one of the first few times they communicate. Otherwise, they pretty much ignore each other most of the time.

Minuted by Middling Industries, 2013

HAEE:

Why do you write a book on middlings?

R.S. VERN:

I live in a small country where majority of the population is middle class. Many of us work hard in pursuit of a better livelihood, or migrate in search of a dream/ career. Sometimes, we end up feeling bored, confused, alone, unattached, and unachieved. But I would like to think this is perfectly all right and a lot of us feel the same way. After all, life is not about having that perfect ending, but having that extraordinary journey.

HAEE:

What's your definition of middlings?

R.S. Vern:

Middlings live in the city. They have a comfortable standard of living and rely on their own expertise to sustain themselves. They place great emphasis on independence and have great concerns for the environment. Whilst they appear well rounded and established, they often have insecurities locked within.

HAEE:

When did you start writing this series?

R.S. VERN:

I started conceptualising this series during the 2008 financial crisis. I was sitting in a café on a weekday afternoon and I saw salaried men in their work suits and brief cases, gazing out of the window listlessly, seemingly waiting for time. When it was six o'clock, many of them stood up and left as if it was time to go home. I later realised many of these men were unemployed. They needed to either pretend they were going to work so that their families wouldn't judge them as incompetent, or follow a routine which they had become so familiar with. I thought that was rather peculiar and yet, so poignant in this society we live in.

HAEE:

Why do you constantly have rules that your characters are being subjected to?

R.S. VERN:

Whilst we are all free to make our own choices, we also need a set of rules to live by. And that is the dilemma most of us face. We hate being caged in by rules and regulations and yet, we feel lost and aimless without them. In every new environment, we need a set of rules to discipline our thoughts and make sense of the new. We are always conditioned to adapt at the end of the day.

HAEE:

Why do you use me as the protagonist in your series?

R.S. VERN:

This series is about middling lives and it is something that is quite close to my heart. I feel it is less brutal to see life through the eyes of a cat.

HAEE:

So are you writing you as me, if you know what I mean?

R.S. VERN:

Yes, I know what you mean and the answer is yes and no. I am somewhat very much like you - independent, restless, and free-spirited. But I am somewhat like Tom and Jane too, as I am often bounded by the demands and realities of living in the city I am in.

HAEE:

In Part 1 "Haee The Cat with a Crooked Tail", Tom and Jane are portrayed as middling characters who constantly wish they were doing something else. Is there an underlying message behind this?

R.S. VERN:

Middlings often ask themselves this question: "Are we not as happy as those who are much better off in this world?" We often find ourselves doing something we may not enjoy best because of the realities and demands of living in the city. I think most of us have a secret desire to live a life that is less demanding and more frivolous.

HAEE:

Just for the record, I do not have a long and crooked tail. Why does my character in your book have a long and crooked tail?

R.S. Vern:

Middlings are never perfect people. All the characters in this series have physical imperfections about them. You have a long and crooked tail. Tom has claw-like hands. Jane has chronic hives. Whie has a big red nose that almost covers her face. It is fiction after all.

Haee:

Thanks for the session. Chill.

R.S. Vern:

Okaaaayy.... that's a bit abrupt. But chill anyway.

An Interview with Haee

This is an interview with Haee by R.S. Vern. Silent and pensive most of the time, this is the first time he has granted an interview to a human being. After the interview, R.S. Vern revealed she thought she knew Haee, but actually, she does not now. The interview ended abruptly with Haee walking away.

Minuted by Middling Industries, 2014

R.S. VERN:

So how do you feel now that people are reading about you?

HAEE:

*blink *blink *purr.... Life goes on. I still eat, sleep, poo, daydream, wait for death.

R.S. VERN:

What's your favourite drink?

HAEE:

Root-beer. Preferably with a scoop of vanilla ice cream.

R.S. Vern:

What's your favourite food?

Haee:

Chopped chicken liver is my all-time favourite. Occasionally, I like nibbling on prickly plants... just to tickle my throat.

R.S. Vern:

Favourite song?

Haee:

Currently, it's "High Hopes" by Pink Floyd.

R.S. Vern:

What's your favourite TV channel?

Haee:

I don't have a choice in programming.

R.S. Vern:

Do you have an all-time favourite book?

Haee:

"The Outsider" by Albert Camus. I am intrigued by the character of Meursault. I respect anyone who would die for truth, even if the truth is hard to bear or accept. When Meursault was sentenced to death in the end, he told the chaplain he had naturally wished for another life sometime. But it meant nothing more than wishing he was rich or could swim faster. It was the same thing and he said finally, "One which would remind me of this life." That's one intriguing statement.

R.S. VERN:

Any literary hero?

HAEE:

Quasimodo, the tragic hero from Notre Dame de Paris by Victor Hugo. He's romantically humane beneath that totally deformed outer body.

R.S. VERN:

Is there a particular book you enjoy reading during rainy days?

HAEE:

"One day in the life of Ivan Denisovich" by Alexander Solzhenitsyn. Reading it always reminds me the importance of simple things like a piece of bread, a book, a match, a string and most importantly, what freedom means.

R.S. VERN:

What do you plan to read next?

HAEE:

I was just picking up "Down and Out in Paris and London" by George Orwell.

R.S. VERN:

Ok. Getting back to favourites. Do you have a favourite colour?

HAEE:

Are you trying to be funny? I'm colour blind.

R.S. VERN:

Em... ok. Sorry... (Embarrassed)

HAEE:

Don't be sorry. There's nothing to be sorry about. I'm still alive.

R.S. VERN:

Oh... okaaaaay. So do you have any favourite food?

HAEE:

You asked me that earlier.

R.S. VERN:

Oh... sorry...

HAEE:

Stop saying sorry.

R.S. VERN:

(Clears throat) If there's one thing you can change about the world, what would it be?

HAEE:

To have better and cleaner air in the city.

R.S. VERN:

Have you ever wished you could be something else other than a cat?

HAEE:

I don't mind being a cat. But sometimes I wish I could walk on 2 legs and not 4. Like you.

R.S. VERN:

Why is that?

HAEE:

Then I can be a bit more normal and perhaps taller.

R.S. VERN:

Huh?

HAEE:

(Rolls eyes)

The interview ended abruptly here as Haee walked away.

Winner of IndieReader Discovery Awards 2013
5 Stars Rating by Readers' Favorite

"an interesting book focusing on the ideas of need versus want, self-fulfillment, and motivations.....I suspect it is one of those books that you can turn to again and again and find different things, dependent upon your mood." - Kindle Book Review

"Bittersweet and seemingly simple, this story embodies the ambivalence the author feels about an average, middle-class existence - possibly mundane, yes, but reassuring in its certainties and not without its own joys." - ilovebooks.com

"a beautifully illustrated and thought-provoking modern-day allegory suitable for older children and grown-ups alike." - Rated 5 stars by IndieReader

About Illustrated Series

For all ages. Illustrated book series "Haee and the Other Middlings" provides an insightful and delightful read at what it means to be functioning, breathing, and living as we are today.

Relatable and endearing, readers of all ages can find resonance in R.S. Vern's middling characters, both humans and cats. Far from perfect, the journey of its protagonist, cat Haee, serves as a reminder that the pursuit of meaning and purpose is an ongoing endeavour, and amidst our insecurities and imperfections, it is natural for our perspectives to shift and evolve.

Through the imaginative world of middlings, R.S. Vern creates a series of 3 beautifully illustrated novels that provokes thought and contemplation about what it means to live in this 21st century. At the end of it, Vern believes poignancy can also be hopeful as long as we continue our search, no matter.

Part I of this series wins the International IndieReader Discovery Award 2013.

About Scribbles from the Middling Cat

"An engaging work of fiction that appeals to readers of all ages by offering a unique perspective on life and the human experience, as seen through the eyes of a curious and introspective middling cat."

Following the delightful, illustrated book collection "Haee and the Other Middlings", R.S. Vern continues with a collection of interrelated entries written through the eyes of its main cat protagonist, Haee.

These scribbles are an introspection of thoughts, musings, and observations that provide a quirky and playful insight into Haee's world and the middling human condition.

Peppered with charming illustrations among short prose, less is more continues to take precedence in the works of R.S. Vern as we continue to explore the poignancy of middling lives in the 21st century.

About the Author

R.S. Vern is the creator of book trilogy series: Haee and the Other Middlings. Part I of this series wins the International IndieReader Discovery Award 2013.

An oddly conflicted soul, she finds herself constantly torn between the challenges of saving the world and the realities of making a living. She calls herself a middling - urbanised, uneased, and most of the time, in a flux.

Haee is a real cat living in her home. Instead of writing as herself, she feels that it is less brutal seeing life through the eyes of a cat.

R.S. Vern holds a B.A. in English Literature, an M.A. in Communications, and a G.D. in Applied Positive Psychology.

www.ingramcontent.com/pod-product-compliance
Lightning Source LLC
LaVergne TN
LVHW010356160826
845677LV00005BA/1300

9789811871054